Sleeping Beauty

Adapted by Amanda Askew

Illustrated by Natalie Hinrichsen

QED Publishing

Long ago, there lived a king and queen who had a beautiful baby girl.

The king could not contain his joy. He held a great feast and invited friends, family and the fairies.

There were thirteen fairies in his kingdom.
All but the thirteenth fairy were invited as
she was cruel and spiteful.

After an amazing feast, each of the fairies presented the child with a magical gift, including kindness and beauty.

The princess had everything she could wish for.

After the eleventh fairy presented her gift,
the thirteenth fairy suddenly appeared.

Angrily, she called out, "When she is fifteen years old, the princess shall prick herself with a spindle and fall down dead!"

The queen fell to the floor, sobbing.

The twelfth fairy, whose wish was still not spoken, quietly stepped forwards.

"My magic cannot break the curse.
But your daughter shall not die.
Instead she will fall into a deep sleep
lasting one hundred years."

Over the years, the promises of the fairies came true, one by one.

The princess grew to be beautiful...

kind...

and clever.

The king and queen ordered every spindle across the kingdom to be destroyed. The princess was never told of the curse.

On the morning of her fifteenth birthday, the princess awoke early, excited. She wandered through the halls and gardens, waiting for the rest of the castle to awake.

She came to an old tower that she had never seen before. The princess climbed the winding staircase and opened a little door.

In a small room sat an old woman with a spindle, busily spinning.

"What are you doing?" asked the princess.

"I'm spinning. Would you like to try?"
asked the old woman.

The princess had hardly begun when she pricked her finger. At that moment, she fell into a deep sleep.

The king, queen and servants had all started their
morning routines and suddenly fell asleep, too.

The horses fell asleep in the stable...

the birds fell asleep on
the roof...

and the dogs snored in
the yard.

Around the castle a thick hedge of roses grew, until nothing could be seen of the castle.

The legend of Sleeping Beauty, as the king's daughter was called, spread across the land. Princes tried to reach the castle, but the thorns would not let them through.

One hundred years passed, and a handsome young prince heard the tale of Sleeping Beauty. He travelled to the castle and walked through the hedge unharmed.

When he went into the castle, the flies were asleep on the walls and the servants were asleep in the halls.

Near the throne lay the king and queen, sleeping peacefully beside each other.

At last, the prince reached the tower where the princess slept. As soon as he saw her, the prince fell in love. He bent down to kiss her and Sleeping Beauty awoke.

The sleeping curse was lifted, and the castle slowly came to life.

Later that year, the prince and Sleeping Beauty were married and lived happily for the rest of their lives.

Notes for parents and teachers

- Look at the front cover of the book together. Can the children guess what the story might be about? Read the title together. Does this give them more of a clue?

- When the children first read the story or you read it together, can they guess what might happen in the end?

- What do the children think of the characters? Is the thirteenth fairy kind? What about the king and queen? Who is their favourite character and why?

- The villain in this story is the thirteenth fairy. Can the children think of any other stories with a similar character?

- At the beginning, do the children think that Sleeping Beauty will fall asleep for one hundred years ? Are the children glad that the prince broke the curse at the end of the story?

- What would the children do if they met an evil fairy? Ask the children to draw or paint their own nasty character.

- What other endings can the children think of? Perhaps the children can act out the story, and then the new endings.

- Many princes try to help Sleeping Beauty, which is very kind. What things do the children do for other people that are kind? Why is kindness important?

Copyright © QED Publishing 2010

First published in the UK in 2010 by QED Publishing
A Quarto Group Company
226 City Road
London ECIV 2TT

www.qed-publishing.co.uk

ISBN 978 1 84835 487 6

Printed in China

A catalogue record for this book is available from the British Library.

Editor: Amanda Askew
Designers: Vida and Luke Kelly